I am an "I Can Read
Underwater Book."

GROUNDHOG DAY

Story by SHARON SHEBAR
and JUDY SCHODER

Pictures by BOB REESE

F
S HE

On Groundhog
Day we watch
and wait

for the
Groundhog
to appear.

Out of his
hole he slowl
peeps

to see if spring
is near.

If he
sees his shadow,

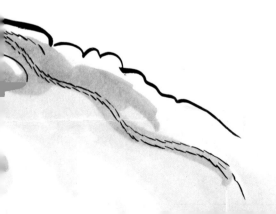

back in
his hole
he will go.

That means
six more weeks
of winter,

with cold and
ice and snow.

But if he
sees no shadow,

out of
his hole
he will climb.

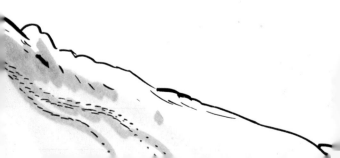

That means
that spring
is here,

and soon
it will be
summertime.